Higgledy-Piggledy

Mabel's World

Enjoy all of the grand adventures
that come with reading good books
and finding new fun-to-say words!

Cristina D'Amico

Library of Congress Control Number: 2005904424
Cataloging-in-Publication Data

D'Amico, Christine.
    Higgledy-piggledy : Mabel's world / by Christine D'Amico.
    p. cm. — (Mabel's world ; 1.)
    SUMMARY: Teaches children how to use a dictionary and have fun with language by exploring a child's new word, "higgledy-piggledy."
    Audience: Ages 3-10.
    ISBN-13: 978-0-9716631-1-4
    ISBN-10: 0-9716631-1-4

    1. English language — Dictionaries — Juvenile fiction.
    2. Encyclopedias and dictionaries — Juvenile fiction.
    1. English language — Dictionaries — Fiction.
    2. Encyclopedias and dictionaries — Fiction. 3. English
    language — Dictionaries. 4. Encyclopedias and
    dictionaries.]   I. Title. II. Series.

    PZ7.D18375Hig 2006   [E]
                       QBI05-600027

Attitude Press
PO Box 16807, San Diego, California 92167.
www.attitudepress.com
First Edition

10 9 8 7 6 5 4 3 2 1
Printed and bound in Canada by Friesens, Altona, Manitoba

The design is by Polly Lockman at www.lockmandesign.com

Higgledy-Piggledy

Mabel's World

Written by Christine D'Amico
Illustrated by Darcy Bell-Myers

ATTITUDE press, Inc.

To my mom and her two sisters—three inspiring women.
You were there when the stories began and have been my biggest
supporters throughout. Thank you! ~Christine

To my dear sweet girl, Vanessa, and to my adorable boy, Rowan. You are my inspiration and my delight!
This book is for you. Now, promise me that after we're done reading it,
you'll go right to bed like good little children! Love, Mama. (A.K.A. Darcy Bell-Myers)

It was her first day of school, and already Mabel had learned something she couldn't wait to tell her family. It was a new word. A wonderful, amazing, and tongue-tantalizing word. Her teacher had used it so many times Mabel had lost count. It made her giggle every time she heard it. She had never heard a word as silly as this one before. Mabel was sure her family would love it.

She didn't have to wait long to use it. Minutes after arriving home, Porkchop, her sleepy old tabby cat, knocked over a vase of blue and white hydrangeas. The kitchen floor was a chaotic sea of water, glass, leaves, and petals. With every step poor Porkchop took to get out of the mess, he carried bits of petals and paw-shaped pools of water with him.

The crash brought Mom running.
"What on earth happened?" she asked.
"Porkchop knocked the vase off the table and created a higgledy-piggledy mess." There it was. She had said it! Mabel smiled. She just loved saying that word.

But before she could think
another thought, her mother had
her by the arm and was marching
her upstairs.

"Mabel, I've been a mom long enough to know an expression like that means you had something to do with that mess. Now you can take responsibility for cleaning it up." Ignoring Mabel's protests and denials, her mom piled rags high into Mabel's arms and sent her downstairs to clean up.

Mabel mopped up the water while her mother swept up the glass. This was more higgledy-piggledy than she had planned on.

Once the mess was cleaned up, Mabel and her mom sat down out on the back porch with a snack to talk about her first day at school. Mabel had just begun to tell her mother about all of the exciting things when her older sister Annabelle burst onto the porch.

"Moooom! I'm trying to make brownies for my soccer team, and I can't find the right pan!" she said.

Mabel's mom went into the kitchen. Annabelle was three years older than Mabel and had already had many first days of school. Mabel was pretty sure there wasn't anything higgledy-piggledy about Annabelle's first day back at school. Just the idea of that word made Mabel smile again. But before she could think another thought, she heard her mom yell, "Annabelle, what in the world were you thinking?"

Mabel jumped up off the couch and peered into the kitchen to find five of her sister's soccer buddies milling about. The floor was covered in brown spots of brownie batter and soccer mud.

Pans, each covered in a layer of uncooked brownie, were either precariously perched on the edge of the kitchen table or dangerously dangling from the hands of a fellow team member. Several soccer balls rolled aimlessly around on the floor. The whole room smelled sweet and sugary.

Mabel's mother was speechless. She didn't know where to begin. Mabel, on the other hand knew just what to say.

"Now this is quite a higgledy-piggledy situation!"

Her mother's glance bounced across each brown splotch and landed on Mabel. "What did you say?" she asked.

"This is quite a higgledy-piggledy situation," Mabel repeated, now grinning from ear to ear. It was that funny word again.

"Well, I don't know about higgy-piggy, but I agree that we definitely have a situation here, and it is not one to smile so proudly about. Mabel, I suggest that you wipe that smile off your face, or you'll be busy in here wiping up a whole lot more," threatened her mother.

Mabel pinched her lips together, forming the smallest O, and backed silently out of the room.

Before dinner, Mabel walked by Annabelle's room. As usual, the noise inside was all a jumble. There were singing animal voices from her cassette player, electronic talking dolls discussing beach plans, ringing toy cell phones, and random giggles from her Make-Me-Laugh Doll. Mabel stopped at the doorway and hollered, "Annabelle, the noise in your room is more higgledy-piggledy than normal today."

Her older sister looked up from her dolls and toy phones, chocolate brownie smudges still on her forehead. "Mabel," she said, "what are you talking about?"

"The noise in your room," Mabel answered. "I'm talking about the noise coming from your room."

"What did you call it?" Annabelle asked as she stood up and came to the doorway.

"I called it higgledy-piggledy," Mabel said proudly.

"And what is higdy-pigdy?"

"Higgledy-piggledy" Mabel corrected. "It's a new word I learned at school today."

"That's not a real word," Annabelle scoffed. "Did you and your new little friends make it up?"

"No," Mabel said, "It's a real word. I learned it from my teacher." Just then Mom called them to dinner.

"I really doubt that," Annabelle said as she brushed passed Mabel and headed down the stairs.

Mabel walked into the kitchen behind Annabelle. It didn't look much better. The brownie attack was over, but now the counters were covered in stringy pasta and bubbling spaghetti sauce, strainers, and wrappers from frozen vegetables, butter, and cheese.

"Mom!" exclaimed Mabel, "dinner smells great, but you and Dad made the biggest higgledy-piggledy mess yet." Mabel shot a knowing look at Annabelle.

"What are you talking about?" her mom asked. "This is the third time you've said that higgly-piggly thing today."

"Mom," Mabel groaned, "it's higgledy-piggledy. It's the new word I learned today at school!"

"What word?" Dad asked, placing a giant plate of spaghetti on the table.

"Higgledy-piggledy," Mabel said. "My new teacher used it today at school."

Mabel's mom and dad smiled at each other and then at Mabel.

"Mabel," her dad said in a loving voice, "I think your teacher was just having fun with you. Higgle-piggle is not a real word. It's just something people say to be silly."

"It's higgledy-piggledy, and it *is* a real word. My teacher used it lots of times today, and now it's my favorite word."

"Honey," said Mabel's mom, "Higgledy-piggledy is fun to say, but your dad is right. Real words are in the dictionary, and higgledy-piggledy is not the kind of word you'd find in a dictionary."

"My teacher wouldn't teach me a word that wasn't real."

"Why don't we look it up in the dictionary after dinner," said Mabel's father. "Then you'll see that it's not a real word."

"We can look it up," Mabel agreed, "but I know it's a real word."

The rest of the night was a jumble of backpacks, papers, hairclips, and school clothes as Mabel and her family cleaned up from dinner and got ready for the second day of school.

Only after Mabel had been given her good night kisses and lay trying to sleep did she remember the dictionary. Their night had been so higgledy-piggledy that she and her parents had forgotten to look up her new favorite word.

But before Mabel could think another thought, their house broke out into one final higgledy-piggledy moment as her mom exclaimed, "Oh my goodness. Roger, higgledy-piggledy *is* in the dictionary. It's a real word!"

Mabel fell asleep smiling. Her favorite word was even funnier when her mom said it.

Hig-gle-dy-pig-gle-dy /**hig** el de **pig** el de/ *adv.*

In utter disorder or confusion. —*adj.* Disordered; jumbled.

Use the word in your own life:

1. The most higgledy-piggledy thing that happened to me today was _____

2. My funniest higgledy-piggledy experience ever was when _____

3. The biggest higgledy-piggledy mess I ever created was when _____

4. My friend _____ is very higgledy-piggledy when _____

5. The thing I like most about the word higgledy-piggledy is _____

Activities

1. **Color pictures of Mabel:** Photocopy the four color-in pictures at the front and back of the book, and color with crayons, paints, or markers. See how many higgledy-piggledy things you can find in each picture.

2. **Create a higgledy-piggledy button:** Photocopy the color-in picture at the back of the book, color in the button, cut it out and tape it onto your shirt or backpack. Then wait to see who asks you about the new word you learned.

3. **Create a string of new words:** Photocopy the color-in picture on the inside of the dust jacket, and cut out the higgledy-piggledy banner. Color it in, punch a hole in one corner and tie a long string to it. Every time you learn a new word, from a Mabel's World book or some other place, get a copy of that word to tie onto your string. At the end of the year you can see all of the new words you have learned.

4. **Make up your own story using the word higgledy-piggledy:** Think of a higgledy-piggledy situation that has happened in your own life and write or tell a story about it. Or make up a higgledy-piggledy situation that you think would be really funny. See how many times you can use the word higgledy-piggledy in your story.

5. **Talk with others:** Take a poll with people who haven't read *Higgledy-Piggledy* and see how many people believe higgledy-piggledy is actually a real word in the dictionary or just a funny thing to say. Tally up the responses you get, and then post the results so everyone can see them.

6. **Learn about words in the dictionary:** Take out the dictionary, and look up the word higgledy-piggledy. Read the definition as it is written in your dictionary.

7. **Other fun words:** Select other words from the dictionary that are strange sounding and, without reading the definition, write your own definition of the word, guessing by the sound of the word what it might mean. Then look at the real definition and see how close you've come.